JUV/E   Cartwright, Ann.
FIC
         In search of the
         last dodo

$14.45

DATE			

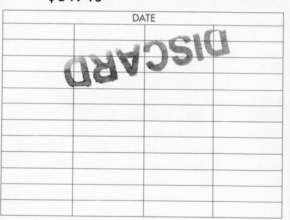

Copyright © 1989 by Ann and Reg Cartwright
B00 74245931
All rights reserved. No part of this book may be reproduced in
any form or by any electronic or mechanical means, including
information storage and retrieval systems, without permission in
writing from the publisher, except by a reviewer who may quote
brief passages in a review.

Library of Congress Catalog
Card No. 88-84118

First U.S. edition

10   9   8   7   6   5   4   3   2   1

Joy Street Books are published by
Little, Brown and Company (Inc.)

First published in Great Britain in 1989
by Hutchinson Children's Books
An imprint of Century Hutchinson Ltd.

Printed in Belgium by Proost International Book Production

IN SEARCH
OF THE LAST
DODO

Ann and Reg Cartwright

Joy Street Books
Little, Brown and Company
Boston · Toronto · London

King Glut was a large, fat, greedy king
who lived in a large, damp, cold castle.
Of all the things he liked to eat, his
favorite food was eggs.

   King Glut had a chef called Adrian.
Poor Adrian! His life was a misery. He
spent all day in the kitchen trying to
think of new recipes to please the king.
He served quail eggs, hens' eggs, duck
eggs, goose eggs, and even swan
eggs. He fried them, he scrambled
them, he curried them and he boiled
them; but the king was never satisfied.
"More! More!" he would cry. "Can't
you try something different?"

One morning at breakfast, King Glut
read in his newspaper that a dodo's
egg had been spotted on a distant
island. "A dodo's egg!" he cried, licking
his lips. "What a delicacy. I must
have it."

He ordered Adrian to prepare the
boat. "There's no time to lose!" he cried.

When the boat was ready, King Glut climbed aboard, clutching a giant egg cup and spoon in readiness for the great event.

"Row harder, Adrian," he shouted. "We must be first to reach the egg."

For three days and nights they crossed the ocean. One morning a great ship appeared on the horizon. It was the *Green Dove*.

"Ahoy there," called the captain through his loud-hailer. "Where are you bound with that egg cup? Not after the dodo's egg, I hope. It's the last one in the whole world and this ship is on a mission to protect it."

"Oh, no, I'm not egg bound," lied the king. "And this? Why, it's no egg cup, it's my crown!" And he turned it upside down and put it on his head.

"Well, be careful," warned the captain. "There are rough seas ahead."

But the king took no notice. He was determined to find the egg and nothing was going to stop him. He should have listened, though, for the sky suddenly turned dark. The sea became so rough, and the waves so high, that Adrian could not control the boat.

"Help!" he shouted, as a mighty wave, as high as a house, crashed over the little boat and turned it upside down. King Glut and Adrian gasped and spluttered and hiccupped and swallowed great mouthfuls of salty water as they were carried away.
Up on top of the wave they went and down the other side.

Just as they were losing hope of being
saved they felt land beneath their feet.
King Glut rubbed his eyes. "An island,"
he cried. "We must be near the dodo's
egg."
　　But the island began to move . . .

It wasn't an island. It was an enormous whale!

A huge jet of water shot up into the air like a fountain. Then away the whale swam with King Glut and Adrian hanging on for dear life.

Even in this new danger, the king could not forget his greed. "We'll *never* be the first now," he spluttered, desperately hanging on to his cup and spoon.

For many hours the whale swam on. Then, through the mist, came a sound. Hoot! Hoot! Hoot! Hoot! It was the *Green Dove* coming to the rescue.

"There she blows," shouted the captain, as he caught sight of the whale.

The captain hauled the wet and bedraggled pair on board. He kindly gave them supper and laid their soggy clothes out on deck to dry. Was the king grateful? Not a bit. He was congratulating himself on his good fortune. Now he would be *sure* to find the egg, with the good captain to guide him to it.

Next morning, as the mist began to
clear, a small green island came into
view. "This is our destination," said the
captain. "Here we will find the dodo's
egg."

"Not if I get to it first," the king
whispered to Adrian.

The captain moored his ship, and
King Glut and Adrian followed him onto
the beach. They found themselves in
a beautiful bay surrounded by tall trees.
"Follow me," said the captain, as he
tiptoed into the undergrowth with King
Glut and Adrian close behind.

Soon the captain stopped. He parted the leaves and there, nestled in the warm sand, was a magnificent egg. A dodo's egg. The very last one in the whole wide world.

King Glut pushed the captain aside. "Mine! Mine!" he cried, grabbing the egg. "Quick, Adrian, boil some water. I'll have it poached!"

But then something happened. There was a rustle, and a crackle, and a pecking sound. A crack appeared in the egg, then another, and another. Out of the egg popped a baby dodo. "Cheep!" it said, as it looked at the world for the first time.

"Ahh," said the captain.

"Ahh, ahh," said Adrian.

Then there was silence. Adrian and the captain watched as the dodo gave the king a sharp peck on the nose.

"Ahh, ahh, ahhhhh!" sighed the king.

He was enchanted. He dropped his
egg cup and threw away his spoon.
"From this day on," he declared, "the
eating of eggs will be banned
throughout my whole kingdom."

"And from this day on," added the
captain, "the dodo will live in peace and
safety on this unknown island."

Then the *Green Dove* sailed for home.
The king was true to his word. From that
day to this he has never eaten another
egg.

And the dodo? No one has ever found
the island.
    Let's hope they never will!